SILLY TILLY

by Eileen Spinelli
illustrated by David Slonim

SCHOLASTIC INC.
New York Toronto London Auckland
Sydney Mexico City New Delhi Hong Kong

ISBN-13: 978-0-545-20735-5
ISBN-10: 0-545-20735-5

12 11 10 9 8 7 6 5 4 3 2 1   9 10 11 12 13 14/0

Printed in the U.S.A.   40

First Scholastic printing, October 2009

The illustrations are rendered in acrylic, pencil, and ballpoint pen on linen.

Book design by Anahid Hamparian

Editor: Margery Cuyler

To the Highlights Family
—E. S.

To Elizabeth, Sarah, Christy, Joey, and Josiah
—D. S.

TILLY WAS A SILLY GOOSE,
a daffy-down-and-dilly goose,
who took her baths in apple juice.

She wore a pancake as a hat.
She tried to ride the farmer's cat.
She kissed a fish. Imagine that!

Tilly liked to tickle frogs

and kick a pickle to the hogs

and hop on top of soggy logs.

She combed her feathers with a rake.

She sailed Pig's pail across the lake.

She sat on Rooster's birthday cake.

One day her friends said, "That's enough!
Enough of all your silly stuff!"
Their barnyard voices sounded gruff.

"No more naps in Scarecrow's pants!

No packing Piglet off to France.

No yodels at the Harvest Dance!"

The weeks went by and Tilly Goose
stopped being such a silly goose.
"Good job!" said Cousin Billy Goose.

It happened, though, that Hetta Hen remarked, "I haven't laughed since—when?—

since Tilly chased the garbagemen!"

"Since Tilly sneezed," said Harvey Goat,

"and blew the fleas from Farmer's coat,

and set his underwear afloat!"

"It's dullsville on the farm. No fun!

I think I speak for everyone," said Horse. "I know what must be done."

And so they did apologize
with quacks and oinks and heartfelt sighs—

to Silly Tilly's great surprise.

Now Tilly's back to her old ways.

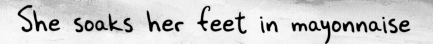

She soaks her feet in mayonnaise

and sleds downhill on cookie trays.

She glues blue glitter on the plow

and turns six cartwheels on the cow.

And all the farm is happy now!